On Market Street

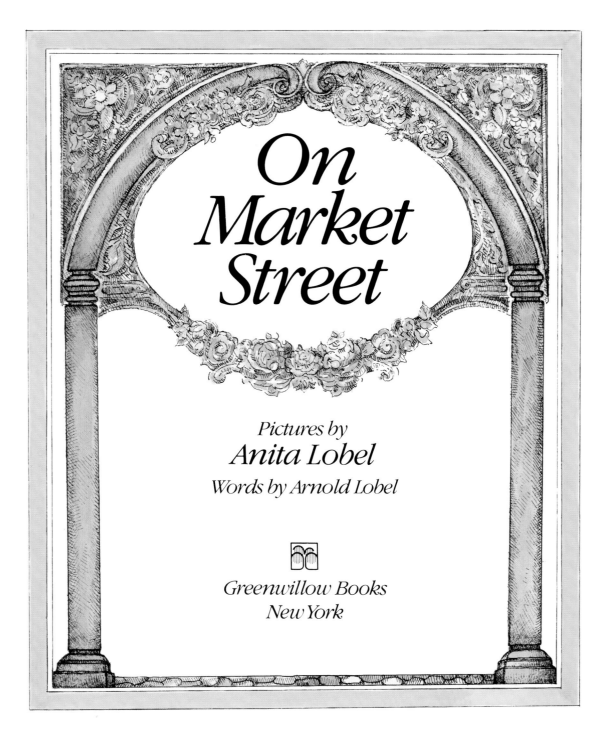

On Market Street

Pictures by
Anita Lobel

Words by Arnold Lobel

Greenwillow Books
New York

Library of Congress Cataloging-in-Publication Data   Lobel, Arnold.   On Market Street.
"Greenwillow Books."
Summary: A child buys presents from A to Z in the shops along Market Street.
[1. Shopping—Fiction. 2. Alphabet 3. Stories in rhyme.]   I. Lobel, Anita.   II. Title.
PZ8.3.L820m   [E]   80-21418   ISBN 0-688-80309-1
ISBN-0-688-84309-3 (lib. bdg.)   ISBN 0-688-08745-0 (paper)

To Timothy and Susan Benn

*T*he merchants down on Market Street
Were opening their doors.
I stepped along that Market Street,
I stopped at all the stores.
Such wonders there on Market Street!
So much to catch my eye!
I strolled the length of Market Street
To see what I might buy.

And I bought…

apples,

books,

clocks,

D

doughnuts,

E

eggs,

F

flowers,

gloves,

H

hats,

I

ice cream,

J

jewels,

K

kites,

L

lollipops,

M

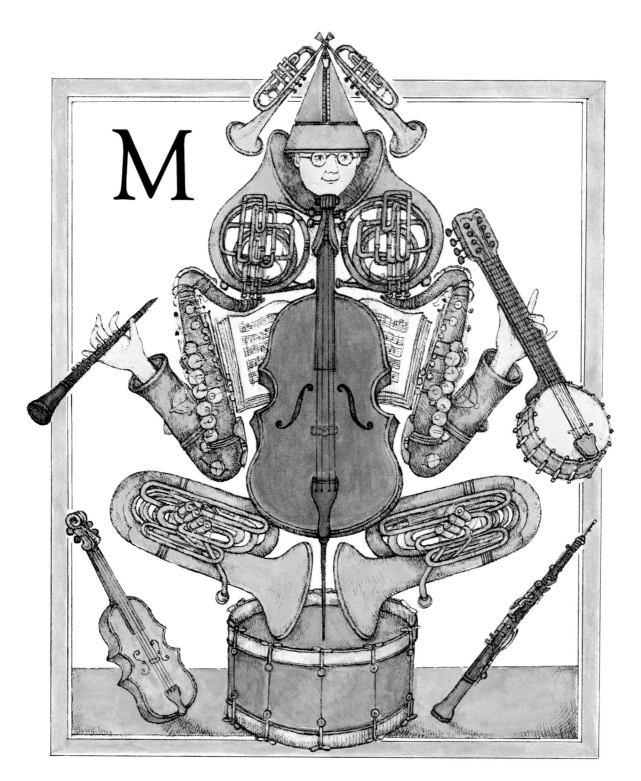

musical instruments,

noodles,

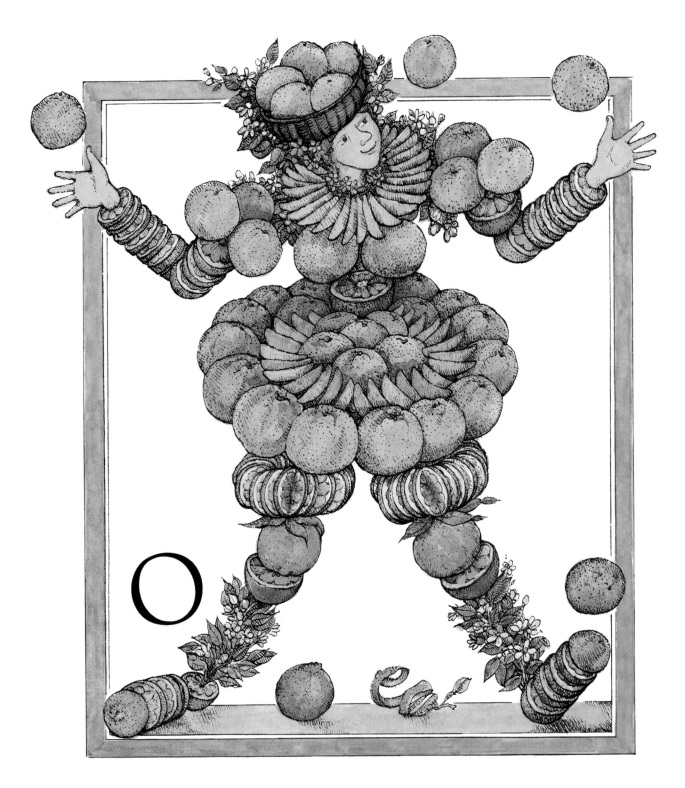

O

oranges,

P

playing cards,

quilts,

R

ribbons,

S

shoes,

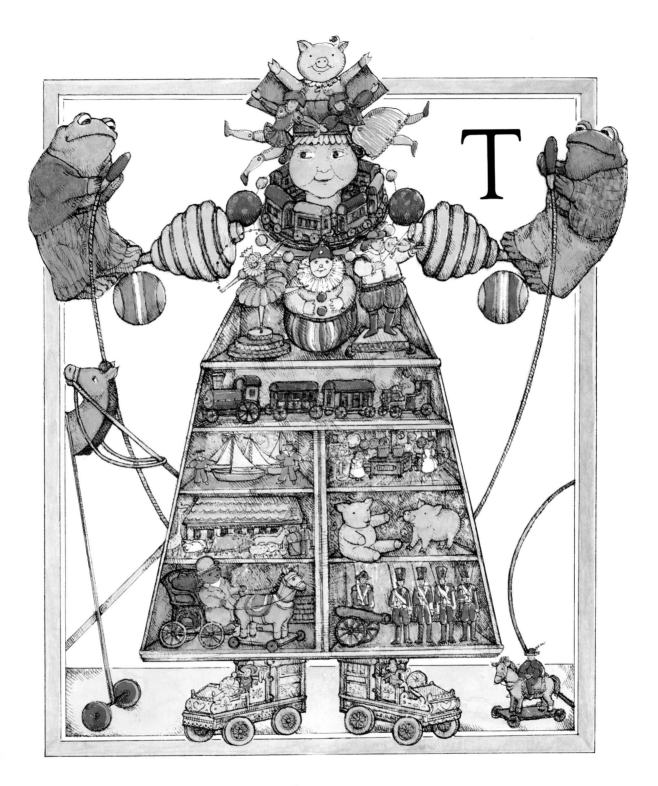

T

toys,

U

umbrellas,

vegetables,

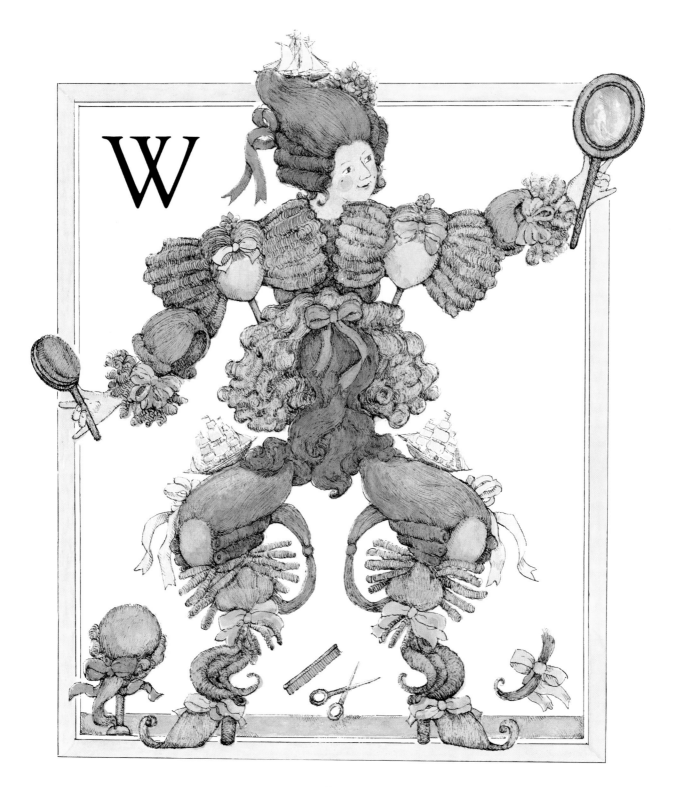

wigs,

Xmas trees,

yarns,

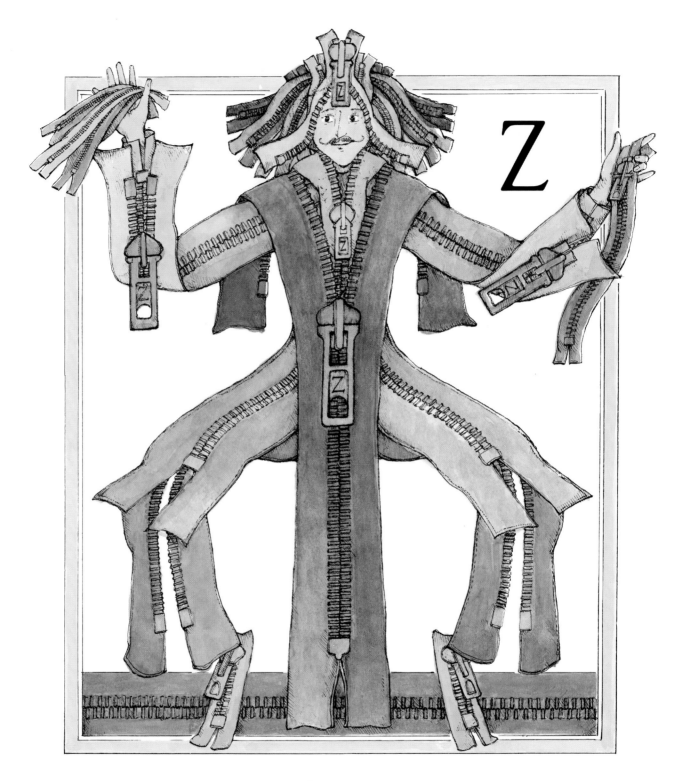

zippers.

My arms were full on Market Street,
I could not carry more.
As darkness fell on Market Street,
My feet were tired and sore.
But I was glad on Market Street,
These coins I brought to spend,
I spent them all on Market Street…

…on presents for a friend.

Anita and *Arnold* *Lobel*,
after many years as separate
artistic entities, say that there is
great joy in collaboration.
The first book on which they
joined their talents was How
the Rooster Saved the Day. *This*
was followed by A Treeful of
Pigs, *an ALA Notable Book.* On
Market Street *was inspired*
by the Children's Book Week
poster which Anita Lobel
created in 1977.